All Ladybird books are available at most bookshops, supermarkets and newsagents, or can be ordered direct from:
Ladybird Postal Sales PO Box 133 Paignton TQ3 2YP England
Telephone: (+44) 01803 554761   *Fax:* (+44) 01803 663394

A catalogue record for this book is available from the British Library

Published by Ladybird Books Ltd
A subsidiary of the Penguin Group
A Pearson Company

LADYBIRD and the device of a Ladybird are trademarks of Ladybird Books Ltd Loughborough Leicestershire UK
© Disney MCMXCVII

Disney's

THE
LION KING

Ladybird

As the sun rose over the vast African plains, its rays touched every corner of the Pride Lands, the home of the lions. In the distance, a great rock stood out against the deep blue sky.

It was going to be a great day in the Pride Lands. King Mufasa had invited all the animals from miles around to celebrate the birth of his son, Simba.

Now, in the cool sweet air of the early morning, the animals were gathering. They were arriving in ones and twos and in little groups. Every giraffe, every monkey, every elephant was there. This was one occasion they weren't going to miss.

Mufasa was already at Pride Rock with his queen, Sarabi, and Simba. He had been up early checking to make sure that all was well in his kingdom.

"You know, Sarabi," he said now, "the more I look at Simba, the more perfect I think he is. Even when he's asleep, his little face looks wise. He's going to be a great king…"

Sarabi smiled back at him, then they both turned to gaze fondly at their baby.

It was Rafiki who always had the honour of first showing a new prince.

"Be careful with our little one," said Sarabi, as the wise old baboon picked up the baby lion.

"Don't worry, I will," replied Rafiki. He turned to the king. "Mufasa, your son looks just like you. Let's hope he will be as clever."

Pride Rock could be seen from every part of the Pride Lands. Rafiki stood on top of the Rock and raised Simba high above his head so all could see. Cheers rose from the plains as everyone joined in the welcome.

Years before, when Mufasa was a baby, Rafiki had held him up in the very same way, in the very same place. It was all part of the great Circle of Life.

King Mufasa was pleased – the morning ceremony had gone well. Only one thing had spoiled it for him – his brother Scar hadn't turned up to pay his respects.

Mufasa went to see him. "Scar, why didn't we have the pleasure of seeing you this morning?"

"Oh, was it today that *hairball* you are so proud of was being presented to the kingdom?" sneered Scar. "I must have forgotten." He had always hated being only second in line for the throne – and now he was third!

Scar's jealousy had always annoyed Mufasa, and today was no different. "You forget you are speaking to your king!" he said furiously.

"No, I *never* forget that," said his brother.

Time passed, and Simba grew. Mufasa often took his son to the top of the Rock, to look out over the vast Pride Lands.

He told him proudly, "Wherever light touches, that's my kingdom, Simba. Some day, you will be king instead."

"And that place in the shadows – is that ours as well?" asked his son.

"No, that doesn't belong to us. It's beyond our borders. You must *never* go there, Simba."

Zazu, the king's adviser, sometimes went with Mufasa and Simba on their trips round the Pride Lands. When he saw anything unusual as he flew here and there, he told the king about it.

One morning he wheeled in the air and flew swiftly back to join them. "Sir, come quickly. Hyenas have just crossed into the Pride Lands," he said, panting.

"Zazu, take the little one back to the Rock. I must go and see what's going on," said the king.

"Can't I come with you, Father?" asked Simba.

"No," said Mufasa. "It's much too dangerous." And he rushed away.

A short time later Simba met Scar on Pride Rock.

"Uncle Scar, guess what?" said Simba. "I shall be king one day, and Father's shown me our whole kingdom!"

"Really?" smiled Scar, who suddenly had a nasty idea. "Did he show you the part in the shadows?"

"No, I'm not allowed to go there," said Simba.

"Quite right. Only the *bravest* lions visit the elephant graveyard. Oops, I shouldn't have told you that! Anyway, it's far too dangerous for you," said Scar.

An elephant graveyard? thought Simba. *How exciting!*

Simba dashed off to find his best friend, Nala. He found her with her mother, Sarafina, and Queen Sarabi.

"Nala, hurry up! I want to show you a terrific place I've found," he said.

"I won't be long," she replied. "Mother has almost finished washing me. At least, I hope so!"

"Just where is this terrific place, Simba?" his mother asked him.

"Er, near the waterhole," lied Simba. He knew his Uncle Scar would be angry if he told the truth.

"All right," said Sarabi, "as long as Zazu goes with you. And don't do anything silly."

"Oh Zazu, you don't need to come with us," said Simba.

"It's the king's orders," replied Zazu. "There's no question of letting you go by yourselves."

Simba whispered in Nala's ear, "We've got to lose him. I want to take you somewhere we're not allowed to go!"

Nala thought this was exciting. They raced ahead of Zazu and hid behind some thick bushes. Zazu couldn't see them at all, even when he flew overhead.

Simba was pleased. "Now we're on our own, we can look for the elephant graveyard," he said.

"I think we've found it," said Nala, pointing ahead to where a huge elephant skull appeared in the gloom.

Suddenly they heard a wicked laugh. Licking their lips, three hyenas were creeping towards the two cubs.

There was a flash of wings – Zazu had found them again. "Run for your lives," he cried…

Then a huge, terrifying roar filled the air. It was Mufasa, racing to the rescue.

He knocked the hyenas to the ground, then stood over them with bared teeth "Don't let me catch you again! I will let you live this time, but next time – watch out!" he growled.

Caught between his powerful paws, the hyenas no longer felt like laughing.

They even tried to excuse themselves. "This handsome lion cub is your son? We're very sorry, we didn't know…" they said humbly.

"Don't you dare come near my son again!" Mufasa bellowed after them as they turned and fled.

The king turned to Zazu. "Take Nala home," he ordered.

When they had gone, there was silence for a moment. Then Mafusa spoke quietly. "Being brave doesn't mean to go looking for trouble, Simba. I was afraid for you."

"Can kings feel frightened?" asked Simba, surprised.

"Of course," said his father. "I will tell you a secret my father once told me. When you feel most alone, look up at the sky. The great kings of the past are always there to guide us. One day, I shall be there as well."

16

Later, Scar went to see the hyenas. "You are complete fools!" he told them furiously. "I gave you the perfect chance to get rid of that pest Simba, and his father as well, and you bungled it!"

The hyenas said nothing. They were remembering Mufasa's teeth. Scar sighed. "I suppose I'll just have to get rid of them myself."

"That would be great," cried one of the hyenas. "Then there wouldn't be a king any more."

"Of course there would, fool. The king would be me! Listen, if you do as I tell you, we can have all the riches of the kingdom. I've just thought of another plan…"

Next morning Scar led Simba down into a deep gorge.

"Why have we come here, Uncle Scar?" asked Simba.

"Your father has forgiven you for disobeying him, and he has a wonderful surprise for you," replied Scar.

"A surprise!" said Simba. "I love surprises. What's going to happen?"

"For the moment, all you have to do is stay on that rock until the surprise arrives." And Scar dashed off – to tell the hyenas to put his plan into action.

Poor Simba! How could he know that he was caught in a trap? Scar was hoping that Mufasa would come to save his son – and he would be rid of them forever.

Simba waited obediently, wondering what the surprise was to be.

Further up the gorge, a herd of wildebeest were grazing peacefully. As soon as the hyenas got the signal from Scar, they charged into the herd. Frightened, the animals began to stampede – straight towards Simba.

"Help, Father, help!" he cried as they came thundering along. He leapt up into a dry tree and clung desperately to a branch. Then the branch suddenly cracked!

Mufasa and Zazu weren't far away, and they noticed the dust rising from the gorge.

"Quick, Mufasa!" yelled Scar, appearing from behind a rock. "There's a stampede – and Simba's trapped down there."

Mufasa wasted no time. "I'm coming, son," he shouted, leaping into the gorge. He grabbed the terrified cub in his mouth and carried him to a high rock. There Simba would be safe from the terrible horns and hooves.

But Mufasa wasn't safe! He was knocked down by a galloping wildebeest. Injured and in pain, he tried to pull himself up out of the gorge.

His brother was waiting at the top of the cliff, gloating as he watched. It had been a good plan!

Mufasa looked up and saw him. "Scar, help me," he panted.

Scar had waited a long time for his revenge. He leaned over and snarled, "Long live the king!" Then he gave Mufasa a deadly shove.

The king fell slowly down the cliff and crashed to the ground, lifeless.

All was quiet at last in the gorge. Simba climbed carefully down from his safe rock to see his father lying there, his eyes closed.

"Father, Father, please wake up and speak to me," cried Simba. "Wake up, Mother's waiting for us…"

Mufasa didn't move. He would never move again.

Simba sat down and looked at him. He understood now – he no longer had a father. The great Lion King was gone.

Someone spoke. "Simba, what have you done?"

"Uncle Scar, it was an accident. He came to save me, and then he fell..."

"That may be, Simba. But the king is no more, and it's your fault!"

"What can I do, Uncle Scar?" wailed Simba.

"You haven't much choice," said Scar. "How could your mother ever forgive you for what you have done?"

"But..."

"There's no argument. You'll have to go away – as far as possible. And you must never return."

Unhappy and confused, Simba fled.

Then Scar turned to the hyenas who followed him like a shadow. "Get rid of him for good!" he ordered.

A little later, the wicked Scar called the lions together
to hear his speech. "Our land has just seen two tragedies,
and it is with a sad heart that I become king," he said
solemnly. "The end of my brother Mufasa, and the
disappearance of my nephew Simba, have caused me
great unhappiness." He paused, and the lions looked
back at him without speaking. Sarabi, Nala and the other
lionesses were weeping bitterly.

"However, our country must rise above this double
shock. We shall move into a new era where lions and
hyenas – at long last – will be enemies no more."

Rafiki turned his back on Scar and walked away. He
didn't believe a word of it.

Following his evil uncle's advice, Simba had gone a long long way from home. The hyenas had soon tired of following him, and had turned back. The sun was growing hotter and hotter. At last, weak from hunger and thirst, he fell to his knees and fainted.

When Simba opened his eyes, he found he was not alone – a meerkat and a warthog were standing over him looking worried.

"You were in trouble," said the warthog. "We saved your life!"

"I'm hungry," Simba said to his two new friends who were called Pumbaa and Timon. "Is there anything to eat round here?"

Timon smiled. "On the menu today, we have creamy grubs and juicy bugs, very tasty. They melt in the mouth." He held some up to show the lion cub.

Simba was not too happy about the idea – he had never eaten grubs before. But he was very hungry indeed, so he didn't refuse. And those grubs really were tasty!

As the years passed, Simba grew into a strong handsome lion. Little by little, he had forgotten he was the son of a king, and that his father was gone, and that he could never go home again.

He and his friends went everywhere together. They took life as it came, and enjoyed it. Their motto was: *Hakuna Matata* – no worries.

"Tonight, let's have a feast," said Timon one evening. "I know where there are some of my favourite grubs – in a tree at the other side of the gully. Just follow me…"

And they strolled across chanting their motto, *Hakuna Matata, Hakuna Matata*. Not a worry in sight!

After their feast, the three friends stretched out on the grass lazily.

"What are those little shiny points in the sky?" asked Pumbaa, yawning. "I don't think I've ever noticed them before."

"They are fireflies," said Timon. "That's right, isn't it, Simba?"

But Simba didn't reply. He was staring up at the evening sky, remembering something from years before. A very old memory, from the time he was a very small lion cub.

"Our ancestors are up there, among the stars," he murmured. "They watch over us and guide us. That's what my father once told me..."

Meanwhile, since Scar had become king, life had not been easy either for the lions or for the Pride Lands. Food was scarce, and so was water. The hyenas were taking everything.

Rafiki, the wise old monkey, had carved a picture of Simba on the bark of a tree. *I am sure he's still alive. And he must be big and strong by now,* he thought as he gazed at it. *It's our last chance. I must find him again if I am to save the kingdom…*

The food that Pumbaa liked best of all was a big fat beetle. Whenever he spotted one, he chased it joyfully through the grass.

Pumbaa's big fault was that he was very greedy. And when he was thinking about his dinner, he forgot about everything else.

"If I catch it," he said to himself, "I will share it with Timon. I will keep the head and the body, he can have the legs – he likes sweet things. Simba will have to eat something else – you can't feed three on a beetle…"

He licked his lips as he thought about big fat beetles and how good they were to eat…

Pumbaa was thinking so much about his dinner that as usual he hadn't been very careful. He didn't know a lioness was following him.

She was hidden in some tall grass, quite near him. She too was hungry, and thought the warthog would make a good meal.

Now she crept forward slowly. A twig cracked. Pumbaa turned round, thinking it was Timon, and saw the lioness. "Help! Timon, Simba, help!" he cried, terrified.

The lioness crouched, ready to spring on her prey. Then, before she could move, Simba leapt on her!

Growls filled the air as the fight raged to and fro. The lioness was as strong as Simba – and she was annoyed because she'd lost her meal.

At last the lioness was able to pin Simba beneath her paws. She looked down at him and couldn't believe her eyes. "Simba?" she asked. "Can it really be you?"

The lioness was no other than Nala, Simba's friend from his cub days of long ago.

"Why did you go away, Simba?" she asked. "Things are so sad at home nowadays."

"How could I do anything else?" he replied. "I wanted to get away and lead my own life. It hasn't been bad. Tell me, how is my mother?" he asked, changing the subject. "Is she well?"

"She is well enough, but she has missed you a great deal ever since you left. Oh, Simba, I'm so pleased that I've found you again."

"I'm happy too," said Simba. "You are so beautiful…"

And they looked at each other tenderly.

Simba and Nala had been apart so long they had a lot to talk about.

Nala begged him to go back to the Pride Lands, but Simba refused. When she asked him again, he just said firmly, "It's too late. I could not be king there now."

At last, tired out, Nala fell asleep.

Then someone said in Simba's ear. "Simba, son of Mufasa…" It was another voice from the past!

"Simba, I'm going to prove to you that your father still lives! Just follow old Rafiki."

Amazed, Simba followed the wise old baboon to a still, clear pool. He looked at him and said, "Rafiki, my father has been gone a long time."

"You are wrong! Look into this pool," said Rafiki.

"It's only my reflection," said Simba. But at that moment a breeze rippled the water. When it grew still, Simba stared down at his father's face. "Father?"

"Simba, you must take your rightful place in the Circle of Life. Remember, you are my son and the one true king. They need you. Go back!"

The vision faded. Simba was alone once more.

Just as the sun rose, Nala woke Timon and Pumbaa.

Her big teeth were a little too near for Timon. He shrank back.

"I'm Nala, Simba's friend," she said. "Where is he?"

Timon was puzzled. "You were with him yesterday evening, weren't you?"

Rafiki broke in. "You won't find him here. He's gone back home to the Pride Lands."

"He's gone back!" said Nala. "That must mean he is going to fight Scar! He's going to take his throne back! I must hurry to join him."

Simba was king of the Pride Lands? Timon and Pumbaa couldn't believe their ears!

Simba was already in the Pride Lands, looking down from a high rock. Once this kingdom had been rich, and everyone had been happy. Now, wherever the light touched, he could see dry streams and bare trees.

"Rafiki is right," thought Simba. "Even if my father's accident was my fault I am Mufasa's son. I must learn to be as good a king as he was. And it's up to me to get rid of my evil uncle Scar."

Then Simba saw his mother, and his heart leapt. He wanted to run to her, but she wasn't alone. Scar was talking to her.

"Sarabi, I have given the order to hunt. The hyenas and I are hungry, and it's your job to feed us..."

"Scar, you have ruined the country. There's nothing to eat for miles."

"Don't answer back! Just do it!" growled Scar.

"If you were half as good a king as Mufasa was..."

Sarabi wasn't allowed to finish the sentence. White with rage, Scar knocked her to the ground with one blow of his powerful paw.

There on his high rock, Simba didn't miss one word of that conversation. He thought his mother was very brave. How could he have left her all those years to face this tyrant? How could he have left the Pride Lands to the mercy of that rascal Scar and his evil companions for so long?

"Scar!" he roared, bounding down to face his enemy. "I've come back! You're finished!"

It was going to be a fight to the death – but whose? Simba was young and powerful, but he hadn't had to fight for his life before. And his years of soft living and no worries – *Hakuna Matata* – would not help.

Scar was different. He was much older, but he knew he had to win or die. He also knew every inch of the ground on which they were fighting.

Step by step, he forced the young lion to the edge of Pride Rock. Simba slipped, his legs dangling over the cliff. He looked up at his uncle as his claws gripped the stone with all his strength.

"You look just the way your father did – right before I killed him," growled Scar.

In a flash, Simba understood what had happened to his father. It was Scar who destroyed Mufasa to steal his throne! In sudden rage, Simba pulled himself back onto the cliff top and the fight began once more.

Then Scar tried to trick Simba by turning to run away. When Simba followed him, he turned back and leapt on him fiercely. But they were too near the cliff edge. Scar's leap carried him over Simba – and over the cliff. Uncle Scar was no more.

"Simba, I am proud of you," said Rafiki. "You have done everything I could have hoped for. You have rid us of a tyrant, and you have chased those vile hyenas from the Pride Lands."

"That was thanks to you, Rafiki, because you showed me the way. Now I have one great task left – to bring life back to my kingdom," said Simba.

"That's what your mother wants you to do. She is waiting now to greet the new king. Come," said Rafiki.